Am I Big or Little?

Written by
Margaret Park Bridges

Illustrated by
Tracy Dockray

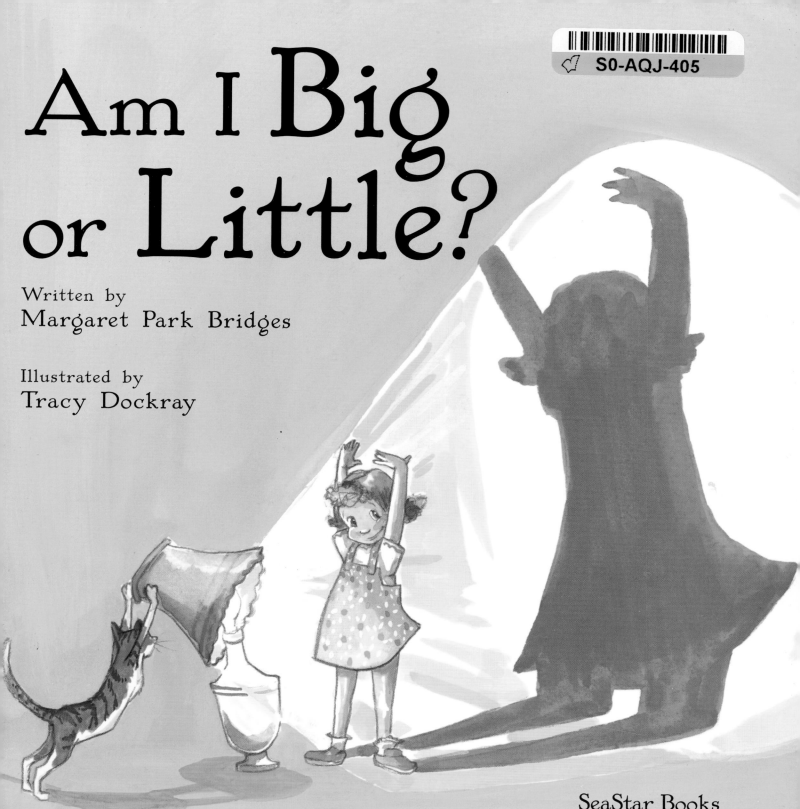

SeaStar Books

NEW YORK

To Harriet,
for her support, generosity, and love
– M. P. B.

For Mark and Lily
– T. D.

Text © 2000 by Margaret Park Bridges
Illustrations © 2000 by Tracy Dockray

SeaStar Books
A division of North-South Books Inc.

First published in the United States by SeaStar Books,
a division of North-South Books Inc., New York.
Published simultaneously in Canada, Australia, and New Zealand by North-South Books,
an imprint of Nord-Süd Verlag AG, Gossau Zürich, Switzerland.

Library of Congress Cataloging-in-Publication Data
Bridges, Margaret Park.
Am I Big or Little? / written by Margaret Park Bridges; illustrated by Tracy Dockray.
p.   cm.
[1. Size—Fiction. 2. Growth—Fiction. 3. Toddlers—Fiction. 4. Mother and Child—Fiction.] I. Dockray, Tracy, ill. II. Title.
PZ7.B7619 Am2000   [E] 00-25825

The art for this book was prepared using watercolor and watercolor pencil.
The text for this book is set in 18-point Colwell.

ISBN 1-58717-019-1 (trade edition)
1 3 5 7 9 HC 10 8 6 4 2
ISBN 1-58717-020-5 (library edition)
1 3 5 7 9 LE 10 8 6 4 2
ISBN 1-58717-147-8 (paperback edition)
1 3 5 7 9 PB 10 8 6 4 2

Printed by Proost NV in Belgium

For more information about our books, and the authors and artists who create them,
visit our web site: www.northsouth.com

Rise and shine, little one.
Time for big kids to wake up.

Mommy, am I **little** or am I **big?**

You're **both,** sweet pea.

But how can I be **big** and **little** at the same time?

Well,

you're littler than I am.

But I'm **bigger** than Kitty.

Right!

You're little enough
to crawl under your bed.

But I'm **big** enough
to reach out and tickle you!

You're little enough
to ride piggyback
to the stairs.

But

I'm **big** enough

to h~op~

all the way down.

You're little enough to bury
your face in Kitty's tummy.

But I'm **big** enough to carry him like a baby.

You're little enough to ride through the park in a stroller.

But I'm **big** enough to make the pigeons fly away!

You're little enough
to stand on my feet
while we *dance.*

But I'm **big** enough
to hold on tight
when you spin me!

You're little enough to have
a tea party under the kitchen table.

But I'm **big** enough to serve my guests *first.*

You're little enough
to want dessert
all day long.

But I'm **big** enough to wait for it.

You're little enough
to share your bath
with a fleet of boats.

But I'm **big** enough to be Captain!

You're little enough to jump on the bed.

But I'm **big** enough
to make it when I'm done.

You're little enough
to share a blanket with your animals.

But I'm **big** enough to save them from the dark.

You're little enough to pretend
you can *fly* to the moon.

But I'm **big** enough
to find my way home.

Well, I'm glad you're still little enough to sit in my lap.

I'm glad I'm **big** enough to wrap my arms around you!

Yes, sweet pea.
You're like a big present
in a little box.

A present for *you,* Mommy?

Of course—just what I *always* wanted!